little Miss Bad

by Roger Hargreaves

Little Miss Sunshine looked out the window and thought back on all the things that had happened in the last week.

Lots of things.

Lots of bad things.

Some things were just a little bad.

Mr Uppity's tennis racquet strings were swapped for spaghetti.

And the cream in Mr Greedy's cream buns was replaced with toothpaste.

Some things were really quite bad.

Little Miss Splendid's shower had covered her with ink.

And someone had painted cracks on the walls of Mr Worry's house.

Mr Worry had been so worried that his house might fall down, he had moved into his garden shed.

Some things were really very bad indeed!

Someone had sawn Mr Forgetful's car in half.

He simply thought that he must have forgotten the other half and had left it at home.

And someone had sneaked into Little Miss Neat's house while she was away on holiday and left all the taps running.

Little Miss Neat got very upset.

Nobody knew who had done all these bad things, but Little Miss Sunshine had a very good idea who was behind it all.

"Little Miss Bad," she murmured to herself.

Little Miss Bad was not good.

Far from it.

In fact, about as far as you can get, which is a long way.

But how to catch Little Miss Bad? This was the question that Little Miss Sunshine was turning over in her mind.

And then she had an idea.

A very clever idea.

The next day a poster appeared in the Town Square. It announced that there was to be a Grand Contest to discover the most mischievous, naughty, or bad trick that had been played in the last week. First prize was a fabulous holiday.

"How easy," said Little Miss Bad to herself. "That holiday is as good as mine."

CONTEST

The day of the Grand Contest dawned. By midday a large crowd had gathered in the Town Square. A stage had been built in the middle of the square.

Little Miss Sunshine called for quiet. "Each contestant," she explained, "will come up on stage and describe their entry and then the panel of judges will decide upon a winner. First up is Little Miss Bad!"

Little Miss Bad could not wait to get on stage.

She was so excited. She had spent all the previous night trying to pick her worst—or best—trick, depending on how you looked at it.

But she had not been able to decide. So she described them all to the crowd—from Mr Uppity's tennis racquet strings all the way through to Little Miss Neat's wet house.

She described them in great detail.

Little Miss Bad was so carried away she failed to notice that the crowd had fallen silent. It was only when she had finished that she saw the expressions on everyone's faces.

She looked to Little Miss Sunshine, who was the only person in the square with a smile on her face, a rather smug smile. It suddenly occurred to Little Miss Bad just what she had been tricked into doing.

“I-I-I was only j-joking,” she stammered.

“Anything more to say?” asked Little Miss Sunshine.

Little Miss Bad looked very ashamed. “I’m sorry,” she said quietly.

Little Miss Bad learnt her lesson that day.

The lesson continued for a number of weeks as it took her a long time to repair all the damage and clean up all the mess she had caused.

Mr Forgetful's car will never look quite the same. Luckily he can't remember what it looked like in the first place.

But nothing she had to do was as bad as those moments standing on the stage with the crowd glaring at her.

It was a very long time before she even thought of doing anything bad again.

And the same could be said of one other person that day …

Mr Mischief.

He slipped away from his place next to the stage and slunk off home, where he breathed a very, very deep sigh of relief!